THIS BOOK BELONGS TO

_____

*In memory of my German grandfather, Walter Harry Seiter,
and his Liebling, my grandmother Alice*

Library of Congress Cataloging-in-Publication Data

Rowley, Deborah Pace.
  The miracle of the wooden shoes / Deborah Pace Rowley.
      p.   cm.
  Summary: Ten-year-old Walter, a German boy, has tried to be grown-up and help as much as possible since realizing that his father is dying, but as Scripture passages and gifts fill his shoes on St. Nicholas Day and the days following, his family receives the help they really need.
  ISBN 978-1-59038-990-4 (hardbound : alk. paper)
  [1. Family life—Germany—Fiction.   2. Sick—Fiction.   3. Christian life—Fiction.   4. Saint Nicholas Day—Fiction.   5. Miracles—Fiction.
6. Mormons—Germany—Fiction.   7. Germany—Fiction.]   I. Title.
  PZ7.R79832Mir 2008
  [Fic]—dc22   2008020624

Printed in the United States of America
Publishers Printing, Salt Lake City, UT

10 9   8   7   6   5   4   3   2   1

THE MIRACLE
OF THE
WOODEN
SHOES

Written by Deborah Pace Rowley

Illustrated by Dan Burr

DESERET
BOOK

SALT LAKE CITY, UTAH

Walter looked sadly out the window. Tomorrow was St. Nicholas Day, December 6. Tonight every German child would set out wooden shoes and wait excitedly for St. Nicholas to fill them with candy, nuts, and little toys.

Every German child, that is, but Walter. Walter was ten years old, and he didn't want to put his shoes on the doorstep. He couldn't fill them with carrots and straw for the horse of St. Nicholas. Not this year. This year his father was sick. Walter watched the doctor and his mother after every visit. Their mouths would pinch together in tight lines, and they would whisper in the corner of the room. Mother didn't say it, but Walter knew Father was dying.

From the day Father collapsed in front of the house after staggering home from work, Walter had tried to act grown up. He searched for hours for a few dry sticks for firewood. He hoarded the candle stubs his teacher discarded at school. He held baby Erika, trying to soothe her listless crying. He dug for forgotten carrots and turnips in the frozen ground of the garden until his fingers were bloody. Walter was grown up enough to know that this year there would be no Christmas.

The tow-headed little boy turned from the window and fumbled around in the cold darkness for his nightshirt. Then he obediently went to kiss Mother and Father good night.

"Liebling," Mother said affectionately as she held Walter's thin face in her work-worn hands. "You mustn't forget to set out your shoes." Walter stared at the floor and left the room without speaking. He didn't want to upset his mother or disturb his father's sleep, but he couldn't set out the shoes. To be safe, Walter opened and closed the front door to hide his rebellion. Then he climbed into bed for the night. ❧

Early the next morning Mother called from the kitchen, "Walter, schnell! Quick! Come and see your wooden shoes." Walter pulled his shabby coat over his nightshirt and hurried to stand by his mother in the bitter cold of the open door. There on the doorstep were his shoes. In his right shoe was a scroll, a yellow roll of parchment tied with a festive red ribbon. In the left shoe were candles of all shapes and sizes. There were enough candles for Mother to finish her sewing at night, even enough candles for a proper Advent wreath. Walter grabbed the shoes and carried them breathlessly into the kitchen. He placed them on the table next to his bowl of gruel and looked at his mother. 🖋

Her face was filled with wonder. She could only shake her head at his questions. No, she didn't know who had filled the shoes. She said it was a miracle. Walter carefully untied the red ribbon and unrolled the parchment scroll. The fragile paper shone in the light streaming through the frosted window.

I am the light of the world: he that followeth me shall not walk in darkness, but shall have the light of life. —JOHN 8:12

Walter read the scroll again and looked at his mother. Tears rolled down her cheeks.

The next morning Walter woke first. He put on his coat and reached for his shoes so he could go outside to find a few sticks for the stove. But his shoes were gone. Cautiously, Walter opened the front door. There were his shoes again! The right shoe held a second scroll tied in a red ribbon. The left shoe was filled to overflowing with sticks, and more wood was stacked against the wall of the house. Walter picked up the right shoe and carried it to the kitchen table where he could open the scroll.

His word was in mine heart as a burning fire. —JEREMIAH 20:9

Walter quietly carried in the wood one log at a time so he wouldn't wake his mother. Then he built a fire in the stove, hot enough to heat the whole house, hot enough to warm his father's bed in the back room.

The third day of the miracle, Walter waited in bed until his mother was asleep. Then he tiptoed to the front door and pulled it open just wide enough to slide the wooden shoes one at a time through the crack.

Now he was up before dawn, creeping to the front door in the dark. He felt like shouting when he saw his wooden shoes filled again. The right shoe contained a scroll. The left shoe held a loaf of bread. Rolls and lebkuchen were wrapped in a cloth. A pail of milk and a basket of fruit and vegetables stood behind the shoes.

The yellow parchment scroll contained another verse from the scriptures.

And Jesus said unto them, I am the bread of life: he that cometh to me shall never hunger; and he that believeth on me shall never thirst. —JOHN 6:35

Walter carried the food into the house. When he closed the door, the baby started to cry. Walter pulled her cradle close to the table and dipped a clean cloth in the milk. Erika sucked on the cloth eagerly as Walter found the same verses in the Bible that were written on the scrolls. He dipped the cloth in milk for the baby again and again as he read.

Walter thought he knew how Erika felt. He couldn't get his fill of the scriptures.

The fourth evening Walter set out the shoes again while Mother watched him from her chair by the fire. She smiled and began to hum the simple melody of "Stille Nacht." After he climbed into bed, Walter could hear her peacefully humming until he fell asleep.

The next morning the shoes were empty. Walter's father was getting worse, even with the warmth and the food in the house. His body was burning with fever and racked with coughing fits. He didn't open his eyes even when Walter sat on his bed and stole closer to softly stroke his cheek.

That same day there was a knock on the door. On the porch were two tall American missionaries. Walter had seen them in town. When they looked longingly at the warm fire, Walter knew he should let them in. One of the missionaries reached into his satchel and pulled out a small parchment scroll tied with a red ribbon. Mother and Walter looked at each other in surprise as the missionary began to read.

I am the resurrection, and the life: he that believeth in me, though he were dead, yet shall he live: And whosoever liveth and believeth in me shall never die. —John 11:25–26

Walter jumped to his feet and pointed at the scroll. "It was you! You are the one who filled my shoes. You gave us the three scrolls!" The missionary shook his head in confusion. "I don't know what you mean. I found this scroll in my shoes this morning with a note to visit your family today. I don't know where it came from."

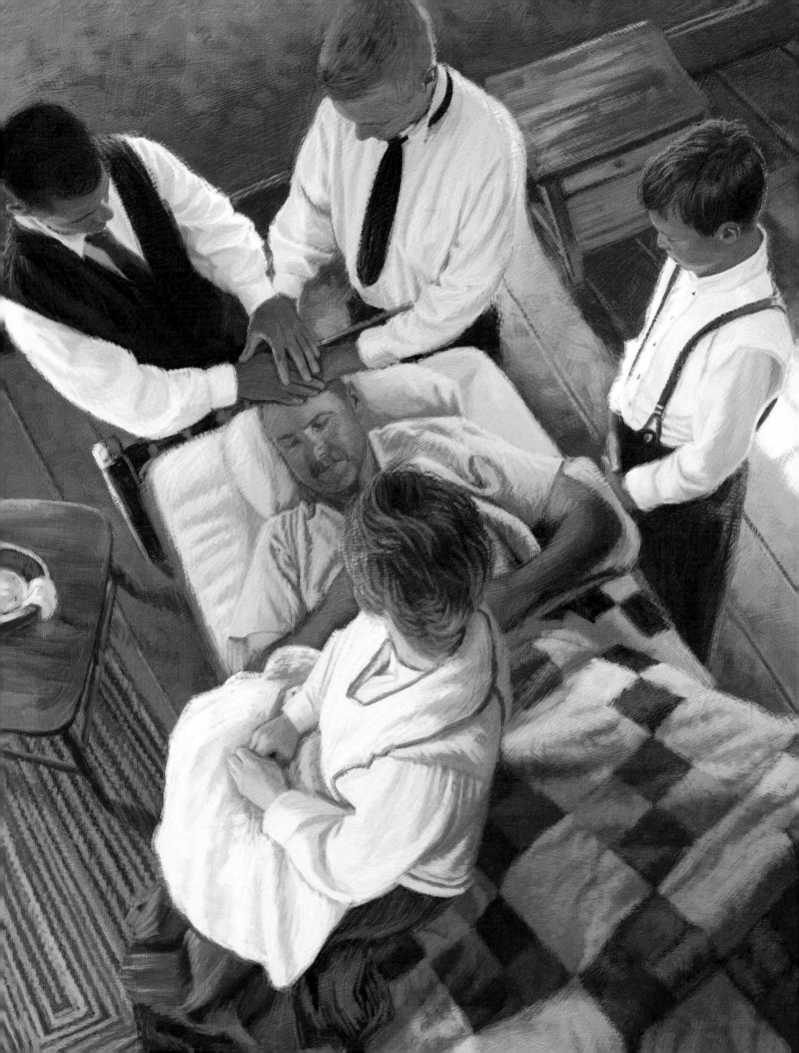

Mother pulled Walter back down beside her. "I think we must listen to what the Americans have to say." The missionaries taught Walter and his mother about a prophet named Joseph Smith, who had restored Christ's true Church to the earth. Along with the truths of the gospel, Joseph Smith had received the keys of the priesthood.

One of the elders said quietly, "I understand that your husband is not well. With your permission we have come to use the priesthood to bless him."

Mother led the missionaries to the back of the house. Walter watched as the elders put their hands on his father's head. The missionary blessed Father through the healing power of Christ, given to all those with faith in Him. Walter felt his heart begin to pound. He had read in the scriptures about the miracles of Jesus as He healed the sick. Walter knew that Jesus could make his father well.

The missionaries finished their blessing. While Mother saw them to the door, Walter stayed in the back bedroom, staring at his father's face. After several minutes, Father opened his eyes, smiled weakly, and reached out his hand to Walter.

The missionaries returned many times during the next few weeks to teach the family. Father grew stronger every day. Walter became a member of The Church of Jesus Christ of Latter-day Saints on Joseph Smith's birthday, December 23. He was baptized in the freezing water of a river near town. Mother was worried that Walter would become sick from the cold, so after the baptism the missionaries took his hands and ran home with him along the bank of the river. Walter felt warm inside with feelings that had nothing to do with running. 🐚

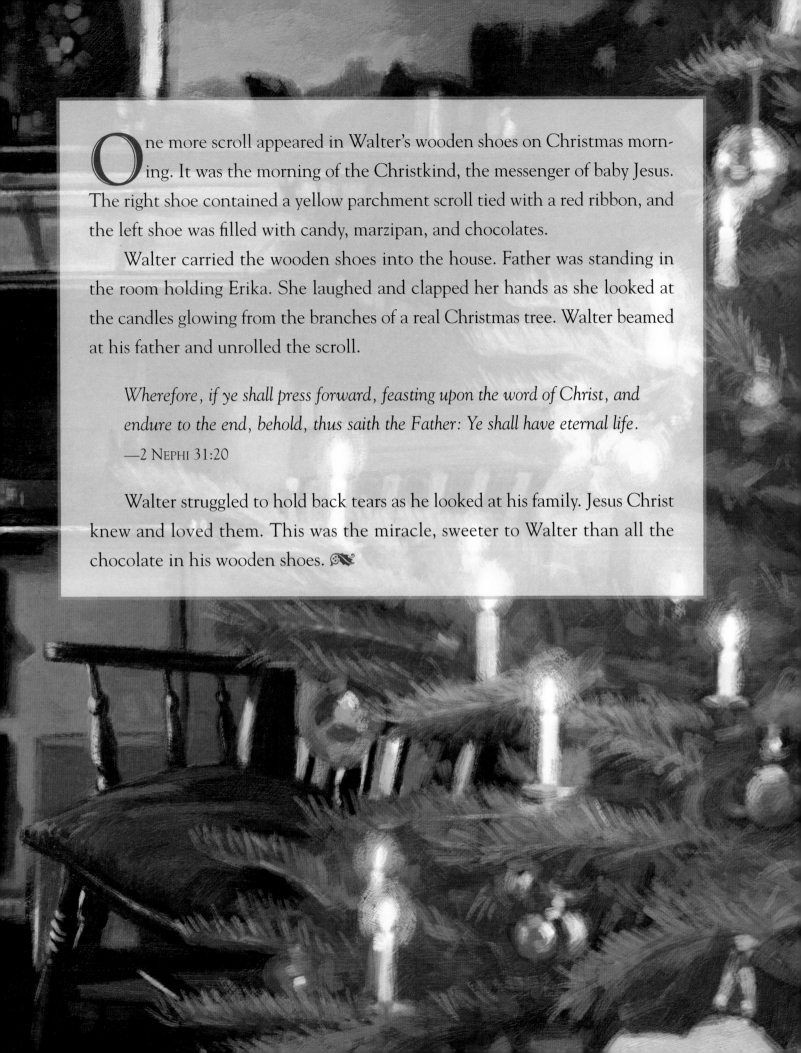

One more scroll appeared in Walter's wooden shoes on Christmas morning. It was the morning of the Christkind, the messenger of baby Jesus. The right shoe contained a yellow parchment scroll tied with a red ribbon, and the left shoe was filled with candy, marzipan, and chocolates.

Walter carried the wooden shoes into the house. Father was standing in the room holding Erika. She laughed and clapped her hands as she looked at the candles glowing from the branches of a real Christmas tree. Walter beamed at his father and unrolled the scroll.

Wherefore, if ye shall press forward, feasting upon the word of Christ, and endure to the end, behold, thus saith the Father: Ye shall have eternal life.
—2 Nephi 31:20

Walter struggled to hold back tears as he looked at his family. Jesus Christ knew and loved them. This was the miracle, sweeter to Walter than all the chocolate in his wooden shoes.

Share the Miracle

You can share the miracle of the wooden shoes with your friends and neighbors this Christmas.

Day 1. Write or print the following scripture on parchment and roll it up with a red ribbon: "I am the light of the world: he that followeth me shall not walk in darkness, but shall have the light of life."—John 8:12. Secretly deliver the scroll with a bundle of taper candles tied with a festive ribbon, or a jar candle with your favorite holiday scent.

Day 2. Write or print the following scripture on parchment and tie it with a red ribbon: "His word was in mine heart as a burning fire."—Jeremiah 20:9. Deliver the scroll on the second night with a box of hearth matches or a bundle of fire starters.

Day 3. Write or print the following scripture on parchment and tie it with a red ribbon: "And Jesus said unto them, I am the bread of life: he that cometh to me shall never hunger; and he that believeth on me shall never thirst."—John 6:35. Secretly deliver the scroll along with a basket of rolls or a loaf of bread.

Day 4. Write or print the following scripture from the Book of Mormon on parchment paper: "Wherefore, if ye shall press forward, feasting upon the word of Christ, and endure to the end, behold, thus saith the Father: Ye shall have eternal life."—2 Nephi 31:20. Deliver a copy of *The Miracle of the Wooden Shoes* and some German chocolates or other treats. Keep your identity a secret or write your family's testimony of the scriptures in a card and sign your names.

Enjoy sharing this tradition as well as other traditions from your unique family heritage each Christmas.

GERMAN CHRISTMAS TRADITIONS

Advent wreath. The Advent wreath began in Germany in the 1800s to count down the days until Christmas. Traditionally it is an evergreen wreath with four candles to mark the four weeks of Advent. One candle is lit the first Sunday of Advent, and each Sunday thereafter one candle is added until all four candles are lighted. In our family we gather around the wreath to sing carols, tell Christmas stories, and pray by candlelight.

Christkind. Martin Luther introduced the idea of the *Christkind*, or Christ child, who delivered gifts for Christmas. He wanted the children to focus more on the infant Jesus and less on other traditions. Over time the *Christkind* evolved and was pictured as an angelic little girl with wings who became the messenger for the baby Jesus. In Germany Christmas celebrations lasted all month long, as St. Nicholas brought gifts early in December and the *Christkind* delivered gifts on Christmas Eve.

Christmas tree. The Tannenbaum had its beginnings in Germany. Its evergreen branches symbolized the eternal nature of God, and its shape directed your eyes toward heaven. In the late 1800s the trees were lighted with wax candles to symbolize the light of Christ. My grandfather remembered being locked out of the parlor all day on Christmas Eve while his parents decorated the tree. At midnight the children were escorted wide-eyed into the room to see the tree magically aglow with hundreds of candles and surrounded with beautifully wrapped presents from the *Christkind*.

Lebkuchen. A traditional German spice cookie similar to gingerbread, *lebkuchen* is molded or rolled out and cut into a variety of shapes.

Liebling. Meaning "darling" in German, *liebling* means "favorite" when it is attached to any noun. My grandfather's favorite pet name for my grandmother was *Liebling.*

Marzipan. A confection made from almonds and sugar, marzipan is generally a paste that can be colored and molded into a variety of shapes and figures. My grandmother made us a roll of marzipan every Christmas that she tinted red or green.

St. Nicholas Day. December 6 is the date on the Catholic calendar to honor St. Nicholas, the patron saint of children. On the night of December 5, children in Germany set out boots or shoes for St. Nicholas to fill with candy and small gifts. Because St. Nicholas traveled by horseback, many children put carrots and straw in their shoes for his horse. Grandma adapted this tradition in our family when we set out shoes on New Year's Eve.

"Stille Nacht." The German title of the world's most popular carol, *"Stille Nacht"* ("Silent Night") was first sung in a village church in Oberndorf, Austria, on Christmas Eve in 1818. The words were written by Pastor Joseph Franz Mohr, and the melody was composed by Franz Xaver Gruber. It wasn't Christmas to me until I heard Grandfather's deep voice with his heavy German accent singing *"Stille Nacht."*